Hooray, it's Christmas today.
I have some gifts to give away.
Gently scratch each gift, then smell.
Guess what it is, but whisper, don't tell.

Merry Christmas,
Momma and Poppa.
Here is my gift for you.
Can you smell it?
Guess what it is.

Merry Christmas, Birdie.
Here is my gift for you.
Can you smell it?
Guess what it is.

Merry Christmas,
Grandma and Grandpa.
Here is my gift for you.
Can you smell it?
Guess what it is.

Merry Christmas, Skunk.
Here is my gift for you.
Can you smell it?
Guess what it is.